The DANDELION Queen

Mr. Optimistic

ISBN: 0989592308
ISBN-13: 9780989592307

DEDICATION

To my wonderful wife, Katie, for without your loving support and belief in me, this book would not have been possible. Thank you for our four children, Connor, Noah, Bryce and Kaylee, to whom I spent countless hours reading bedtime stories. They are my inspiration.

Once upon a time not too long ago, a little girl named Grace was walking through a meadow. The task at hand was not to play but to find the perfect flower to give to her mommy for her birthday.

She looked and she looked, but nowhere could she find a symbol of beauty both gentle and kind. She wandered just a little bit more until her legs were tired and her feet were sore.

Suddenly out of the corner of her eye, Grace did spy a feathery surprise. It was shaped like the moon or even the sun but most of all it looked like fun. Grace thought that she should make a wish because she wanted to share her true heart's kiss.

She closed her eyes and gently blew on the pillowy petals, which flew out of view. Grace stood there for a moment hoping her wish would come true...a new baby brother all dressed in blue.

She opened her eyes and saw yellow flowers everywhere then the Dandelion Queen suddenly appeared. Her gown sparkled with diamonds and gold, her beauty was truly a sight to behold.

The Dandelion Queen spoke in a caring, loving voice, "I am here to grant the wish of your choice. All the dandelions here are from me. I created them for all the world to see.

"All I ever wanted was to be a beautiful flower, to be greeted after an April shower. But all they do is put me down and call me names, on this I do frown. Some may even call me a weed, but I am far greater than that indeed.

"I am a sign of life and wishes coming true and the only way to know this is to simply believe it too. When my pretty yellow petals change into little fuzzy flakes, the time has come for a wish to make. Now make a little wish, any wish will do. The best part of a wish is the hope of it coming true.

"I am happy to be present as I stand here at ease. There is nothing more delightful than a cool summer breeze. I don't always control my direction and path, and I definitely didn't mean to land in anyone's grass. To spread life all around is my given task, so a little compassion is all I ask.

Grace was happy now that she'd seen the Dandelion Queen and heard her story. She knew everything was a part of God's amazing glory. Grace was so excited that she ran all the way home. She didn't realize how far she had roamed.

Mommy asked Grace about her day, then waited to hear what she had to say. Grace didn't even know where to begin so she thought she would just sing a song about her new found friend.

"Dandelion, dandelion, how beautiful you are, you are more amazing than a distant star. Dandelion, dandelion, no other flower will do, you are a gift from Mother Nature too!

"Dandelion, dandelion, humble and true, I wish the world could see the beauty within you.

"Dandelion, dandelion, you are a beautiful flower, your nature is an awesome power. Dandelion, dandelion, I do see, I also found this beauty inside of me."

Grace jumped into her mommy's arms, the place where she had always been protected from harm. "Happy Birthday Mommy, this dandelion is for you. You can even make a wish on it too." Grace leaned forward to share her wish and whispered it to her Mommy with a loving kiss.

She squeezed and hugged her mommy tight, then hopped into bed without a fight. Just as Grace laid down her head, Mommy knelt by her bed, "Grace I have something to say...You have a new baby brother on the way. It seems like your dandelion wish has come true and you can help me paint the other room blue."

Grinning from ear to ear, Grace squeezed her mommy tight and whispered to her mommy and the Dandelion Queen, "Good night!"

ABOUT THE AUTHOR

Mr. Optimistic was born Leamon Scott III. After serving in the United States Army and earning a bachelor's degree in psychology, Leamon came upon a crossroad where he chose to not just be optimistic but to become Mr. Optimistic. Since then, he has dedicated himself to his role as a husband and stay-at-home father of four.

After countless hours of bedtime stories, Mr. Optimistic decided it was time to write one of his own. The result, The Dandelion Queen, is his debut publication.

Made in the USA
San Bernardino, CA
03 October 2015